Dorothy in Dreamland

Illustrated by
STANLEY TIGERMAN
*Story by Tracy Tigerman
and Margaret McCurry*

RIZZOLI
NEW YORK

First published in the United States of America in 1991 by
Rizzoli International Publications, Inc.
300 Park Avenue South, New York, New York 10010

Library of Congress Cataloging-in-Publication Data

Tigerman, Stanley, 1930-
        Dorothy in dreamland / illustrated by Stanley
    Tigerman; story by Tracy Tigerman and Margaret
    McCurry.
        p. cm.
    Summary: In a dream, Dorothy helps change the usual
course of events in four familiar fairy tales.
    ISBN 0-8478-1393-2
    [1. Characters and characteristics in literature—Fiction.
2. Dreams—Fiction.] I. Tigerman, Tracy. II. McCurry,
Margaret. III. Title.
PZ7.G3636   1991
[E]—dc20   91-7728
                                                   CIP
                                                   AC

Typography by Graphic Arts Composition
Printed and bound by Tien Wah Press, Singapore

Design by Milton Glaser, Inc.

Dorothy in Dreamland

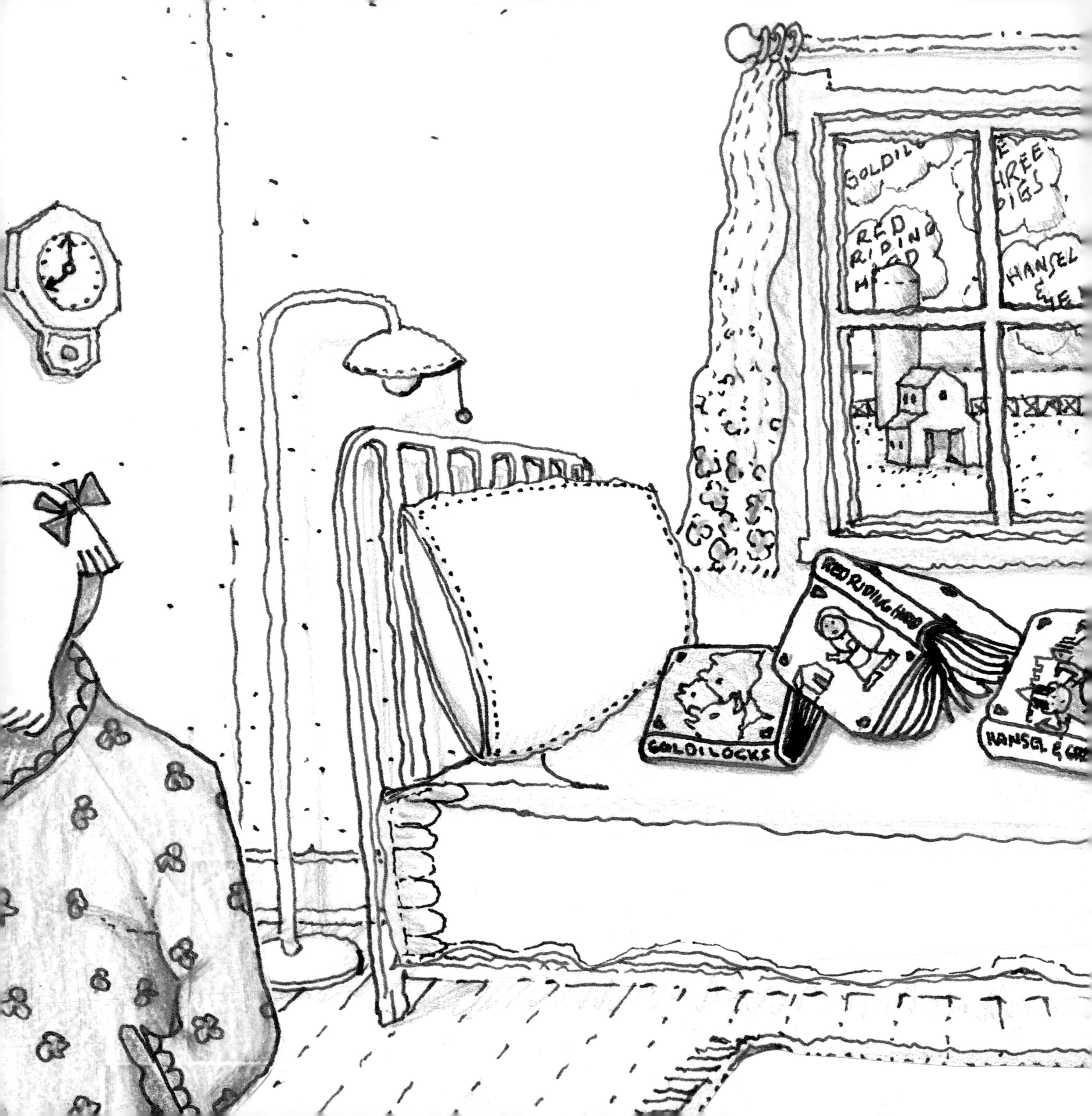
RED RIDING HOOD
HANSEL &
GOLDILOCKS

A WEARY DOROTHY, finished with all her schoolwork, prepared for bed. She hugged her dog, Toto, climbed up into her bed and sat surrounded by her favorite storybooks. She always read before turning out her light, but tonight she was too tired. Closing her eyes, she tried to recall her favorite stories as they were told to her by Auntie Em . . .

OPENING HER EYES, Dorothy discovered she was standing on a path scattered with bread crumbs and leading into a dense forest. Overcome with curiosity, she followed the trail, eating the bread crumbs along the way. Just as she swallowed the last crumb, she heard the sound of children sobbing. Glancing up, she saw a boy and girl huddled together on a fallen log.

DOROTHY knelt down in front of the children and took them in her arms. "Why are you crying?" she asked. The little girl tearfully replied, "Our stepmother has abandoned us here in the forest."

The boy, Hansel, tried to comfort his sister, Gretel, by reminding her of the bread crumb trail he had left, which would lead them back home to their father. Horrified, Dorothy confessed, "I just ate the last crumb!"

"How will we ever find our way out of the forest?" cried the fearful children.

TAKING EACH CHILD by the hand, Dorothy attempted to retrace her own steps. They wandered through the woods criss-crossing many unfamiliar paths until they came to a clearing, where they spied a candy-covered cottage, nestled beside a stream. Tears forgotten, the two children broke loose and ran towards the house. Happily, they plucked gum drops and chocolate morsels off the side of the cottage and stuffed them into their mouths.

DOROTHY, remaining at the edge of the clearing, gasped when suddenly the front door of the cottage opened to reveal a wicked witch hovering in the doorway.

"I'll get you my pretties and have you for my supper!" cackled the witch as she dashed after the children. As the witch chased the screaming children in circles around the house, Dorothy, remembering that witches are terrified of water, ran to the stream where she saw an empty bucket lying on the bank.

DOROTHY RACED back from the stream with the bucket full of water, just as the witch was forcing Hansel into a cage. "Oh, no you don't!" Dorothy yelled and hurled the bucket of water at the witch. All three children watched in amazement as the witch melted away. All that was left was her robe, lying in a puddle of water.

"Hansel, Gretel!" The children turned towards the familiar voice and saw their father standing at the edge of the clearing. With joyful cries, they ran into his outstretched arms.

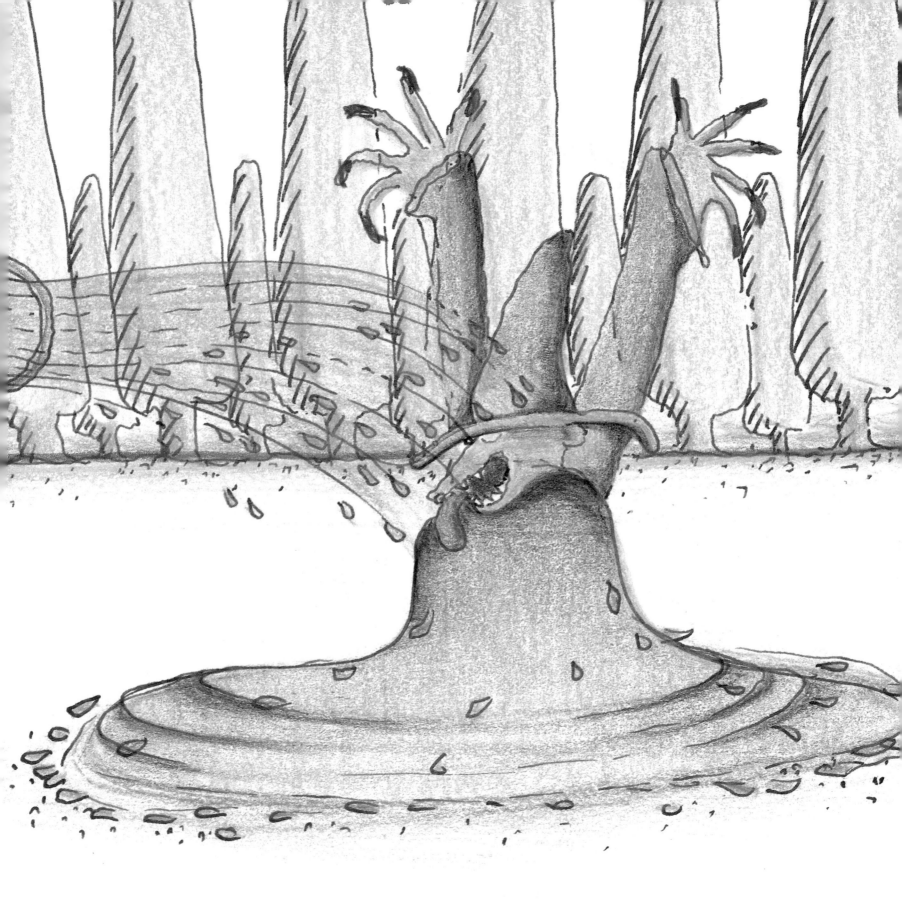

FTER bidding the family farewell, Dorothy continued on her way through the woods. Suddenly, the birds stopped singing and the forest grew very still. Up ahead on the trail, she saw a small, blonde-haired girl dressed in a red cape, talking to a large wolf.

"You just walk along the path until you come to an old oak tree. Beyond that there will be a little blue house with red shutters. That's where my Granny lives and that's where I'm going now."

Peering out from behind a tree, Dorothy saw the sly, hungry look on the wolf's face as he whined, "Thank you, little girl," and, baring his fangs in a smile, slinked away.

DOROTHY WHISPERED to herself, "I don't like the look of this." She ran out from her hiding place in pursuit of the wolf, hoping to reach the grandmother's house before he did. Oblivious to the fact that she had put her grandmother in great danger, Little Red Riding Hood skipped on down the trail.

DOROTHY'S hurried steps brought her to Granny's house ahead of the wolf. She found Granny in her rocking chair on the front porch. Dorothy breathlessly explained who she was and what brought her there.

"We must quickly devise a plan to capture the wolf that will keep you and Little Red Riding Hood from being gobbled up. He'll be here any minute!"

"I'll hide behind the closet door in the bedroom," announced Granny, "and you hide behind the open front door. We'll surprise him!" Together they anxiously awaited the wolf's arrival.

THE WOLF stole through the open front door and, finding the house empty, padded into the grandmother's bedroom. "While Granny is out, I'll just put on her nightshirt and lace cap, jump into her bed, and wait for her plump, little granddaughter, Little Red Riding Hood," he said, licking his chops.

Hearing this, Dorothy jumped out from her hiding place and ran into the bedroom. Waving her arms frantically, she yelled, "Go away, you big, bad wolf!" This so startled the wolf that he became tangled in the bedsheets, tumbled out of bed, and rolled backwards into the open closet.

"Aha, we have you now!" pronounced Granny, as she slammed the door and locked it after him.

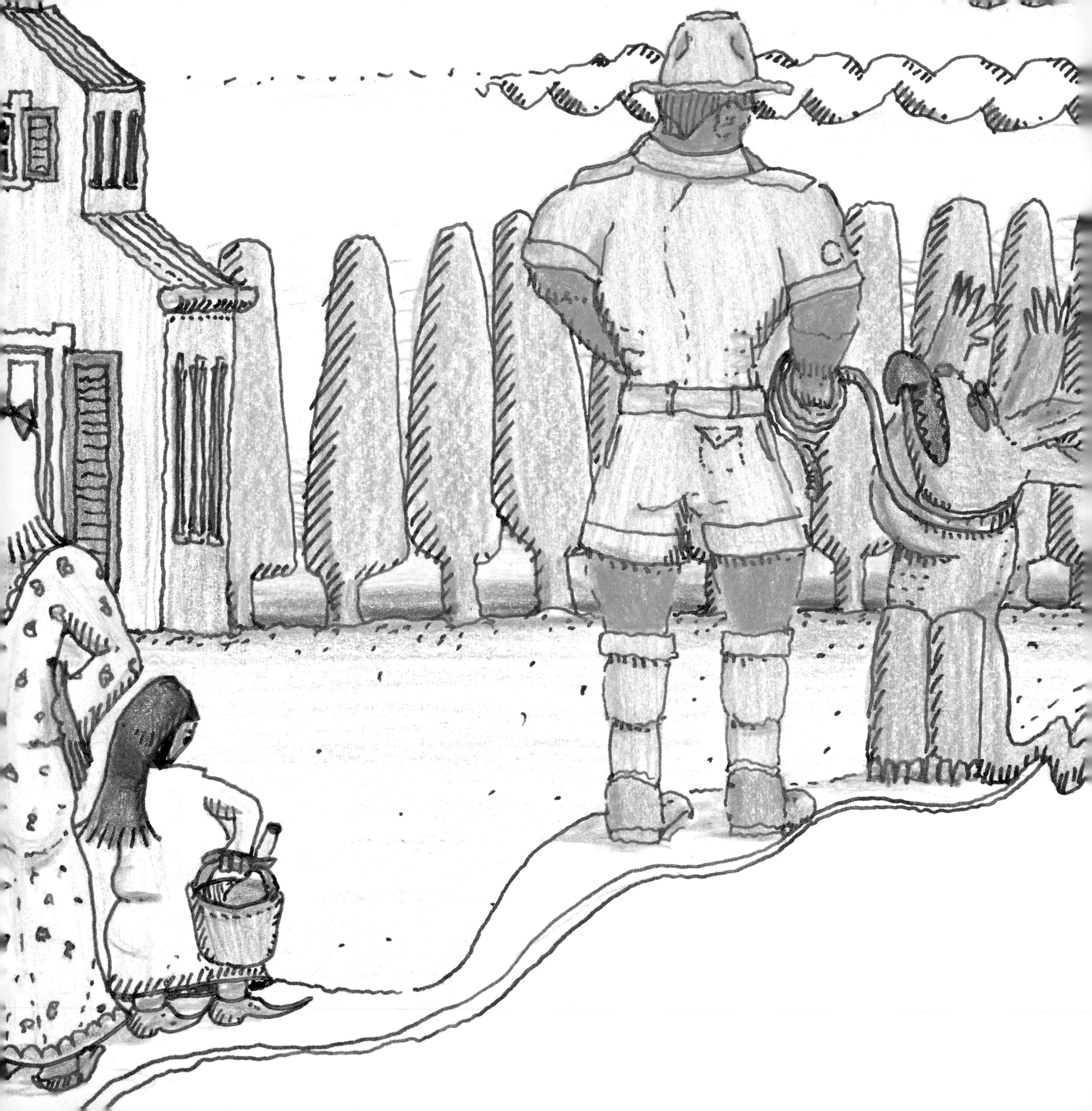

*L*ITTLE RED RIDING HOOD arrived hand in hand with the forest ranger who had heard the trapped wolf howling. The ranger commented from the doorway, "We've been looking for this wolf for a very long time. I hope everyone's alright."

As Granny and Little Red Riding Hood hugged each other in relief, Dorothy asked the ranger, "Where can we put this wolf so that he won't cause any more harm?" The ranger laughed and answered, "I have just the place."

The wolf yowled from behind the closet door, "No, no, not the zoo!"

OROTHY CONTINUED down the path when all at once she heard a rustling of leaves and branches. She stopped just as a little girl with golden hair burst out of a thicket, nearly knocking Dorothy down. "What's wrong?" Dorothy asked. "Can I help you? Why are you running so fast?"

"I'm running from the bear family who chased me from their home because I ate their porridge and broke their furniture," cried Goldilocks. Before Dorothy could stop her, the distraught girl ran off down the path sobbing.

U

NABLE TO STOP Goldilocks, Dorothy decided to investigate the scene of the crime. Arriving at a comfortable cottage deep in the forest, she knocked on the door. A small, sad-looking bear opened it and asked, "Who are you?"

"I'm Dorothy, a friend of Goldilocks," she replied.

MAMA BEAR and Papa Bear joined Baby Bear at the door. "Please come in and have some tea," they said. While pouring the tea, Mama Bear confided, "We did not mean to frighten the little girl. We came home to discover a stranger had eaten all our dinner, broken our baby's chair, and was sleeping in his bed! Naturally we were upset and overreacted. We're sorry and would like the chance to apologize."

"Why don't I go and search for Goldilocks," Dorothy suggested, "and try to clear up this misunderstanding?"

"May I please come along?" begged Baby Bear.

So together they set out.

FOLLOWING the bear's keen nose, the two searchers came to a thicket deep in the forest. Behind it they heard whimpering. An excited Baby Bear galloped ahead. When Dorothy parted the branches of the thicket, she saw Goldilocks kneeling on the forest floor with the bear drying her tears.

"Please come back home with me. My mother and father hope we can be friends," Baby Bear pleaded with the girl. Dorothy watched happily as Goldilocks and Baby Bear skipped home hand in hand.

W

ITH THOUGHTS of finding her way home foremost in her mind, Dorothy set out down the path. After a long walk, she reached the edge of the woods where she stepped onto a dirt road. In the distance she saw three small, chubby figures walking towards her. As they approached, she saw they were three little pigs.

"WHY, HELLO," said Dorothy. "Where are you going?" The pigs pointed down the road where Dorothy spied a farmer's house and a barn and silo. They told her of their plans to build three houses of their own.

The first pig explained, "The big bad wolf has escaped from the zoo, and he wants to catch us and gobble us up. We must build sturdy houses so that we can keep our children safe."

"Will you help us?" asked the second pig.

"Yes, I'll be glad to lend a hand."

ALONG THE WAY, the first pig bought a bale of straw, the second a cartload of sticks, and the third a pallet of bricks. As each pig selected the exact site for his house and started to build, Dorothy walked around giving helpful advice.

She helped the first little pig weave the straw tightly so that no wind could blow it apart.

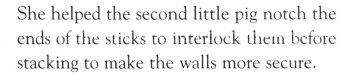

She helped the second little pig notch the ends of the sticks to interlock them before stacking to make the walls more secure.

And she helped the third little pig mix the cement and lay it along the rows of bricks to create a solid wall.

Then she went back to the first little pig's house to check on his progress.

JUST AS SHE ARRIVED, the big bad wolf appeared at the edge of the woods. Dorothy and the little pig raced inside the house and slammed the door.

"I'll huff and I'll puff and I'll blow your house down!" howled the wolf. But the woven straw held tight and the angry wolf stalked off towards the second little pig's house.

Once again, he huffed and puffed and blew with all his might, but he could not blow down this house either. Grinding his teeth in frustration, he ran to the third little pig's house.

Again, the wolf huffed and puffed and blew until his lungs almost burst, but the bricks would not budge.

With his tail between his legs and his head down, the defeated wolf loped back into the forest, never to be heard from again.

As THE WOLF disappeared over the horizon, the three little pigs and Dorothy burst out of the sturdy houses and began to dance about. The pigs formed a circle around Dorothy and then all four joined in a group hug to celebrate.

"Please stay with us, Dorothy, to help protect the rest of the farm if the wolf decides to return," they begged. Dorothy thanked them but declined. "I must get back to my Auntie Em and Uncle Henry. They will be worried about me," she explained.

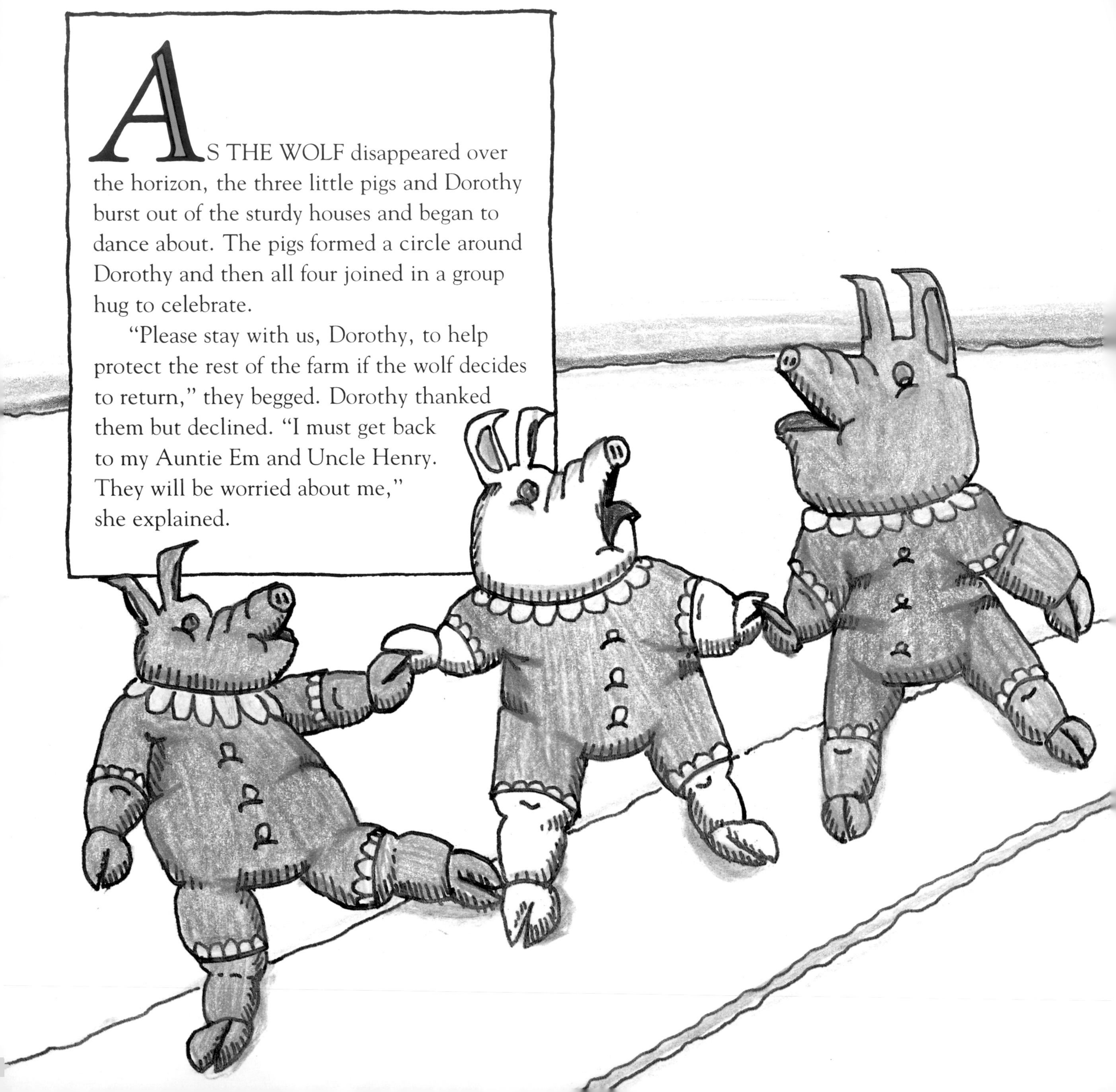

*T*HE THREE LITTLE PIGS waved and waved good-bye until the girl disappeared down the road.

Tired after such a long and busy day, Dorothy was surprised to discover her bed straddling the road. Exhausted, she climbed up onto it. "I'll just stop and rest a moment, then keep searching for a way home," she mumbled to herself as she drifted off to sleep.

*D*OROTHY AWAKENED to
discover that she was back in her own
bedroom. She ran out into the farmyard,
unable to believe she was really home.
Standing at the gate, she thought of all she
had just seen and done. There was quite a
difference between the stories as she had been
told them before and how she remembered
them now. She smiled to herself as she realized
that sometimes your memory of something can
be very different from what really happened.

HANSEL & GRETEL

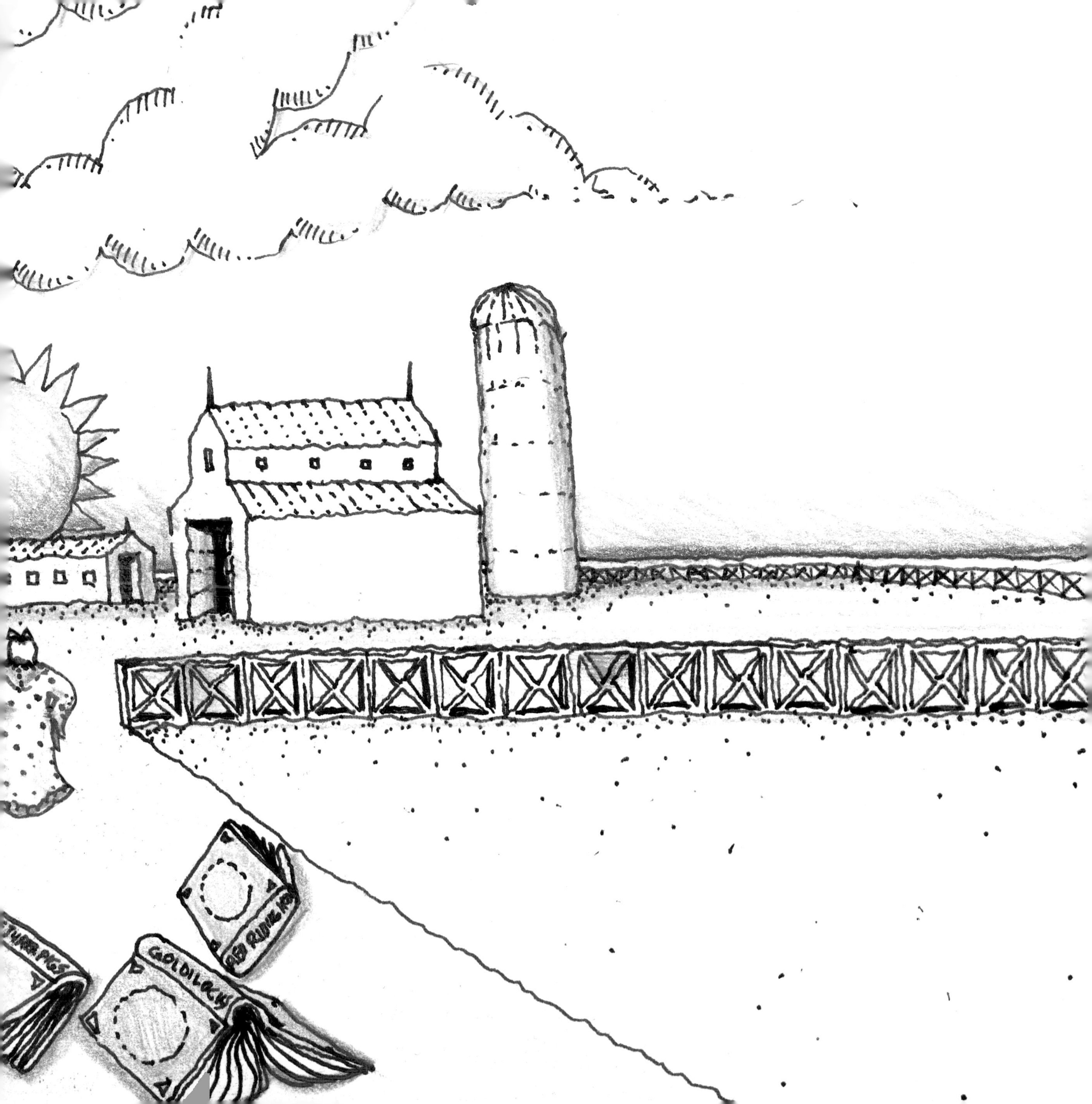
PIGS
GOLDILOCKS
RED RIDING

STANLEY TIGERMAN *received his architectural degrees from Yale University and is currently Director of the School of Architecture at the University of Illinois at Chicago. A practicing architect and a Fellow of the American Institute of Architects, he is the author of four Rizzoli books—and is currently working on his next. Widely published, he has lectured and taught throughout the world, and is the recipient of numerous design awards. His work has been exhibited in museums and galleries both in the United States and abroad, including The Museum of Modern Art, New York. His drawings are in the permanent collection of The Art Institute of Chicago and The Deutsches Architektur Museum in Frankfurt, Germany.*

MARGARET I. McCURRY *received her B.A. from Vassar College in New York and a Loeb Fellowship from the Graduate School of Design at Harvard University. She is a partner with her husband, Stanley, in Tigerman McCurry Architects in Chicago. A Fellow of the American Institute of Architects, she is the author of numerous articles for architectural journals, has lectured and taught at universities and conferences in both the United States and abroad, and is the recipient of many design awards.*

TRACY LEIGH TIGERMAN, *the daughter of the illustrator, received her B.A. in Philosophy from Sweet Briar College in Lynchburg, Virginia, and her Masters Degree in Early Childhood Education from Lesley College in Cambridge, Massachusetts. She is presently a kindergarten teacher within the Campbell County Public School System in Virginia.*